W9-DIU-875

The Magic Passport

by Judith Dupré

illustrated by John Speirs

Table of Contents

Chocolate-Covered Grasshoppers, Anyone?

"Tommy, I don't want to go to your aunt's house after school."

"C'mon, Josie. It'll be a blast."

"Yeah, if you like crazy people," muttered Josie.

Josephina Smith, Josie for short, was the last person you'd pick for a friend. She was bossy and a tattle tale. Unfortunately, her mom was my mom's best friend, so I had to play with her. A lot.

"She's not crazy, she's—" I tried to find the right word to describe my Aunt Matilda. Magical, that was it. "She's magical."

"She isn't magical!" said Josie.

"Is too!"

"Is not!"

"Is too!"

"Prove it!"

"Okay," I said. "I will. Come with me and you'll see some real magic."

"Yeah, I'll bet. I've always heard that she was crazy, and now I'm beginning to think that you are, too."

Josie can't understand why a ten-year-old kid like me would spend so much time with his aunt. But my Aunt Matilda is more fun than getting to the highest level in a video game. More fun than doing a 180 on a skateboard. More fun than riding a roller coaster and eating cotton candy. Aunt Matilda makes me laugh more than anyone else.

She's too busy having fun to care about what other people think. Sure, it's a little strange to plant plastic flowers in your yard, but she likes plastic flowers because they are always in bloom. When you think about it, that makes a lot of sense.

She does what she wants when she wants. If she feels like it, she eats hamburgers in the morning and pancakes at night.

"See what I mean by weird?" Josie pointed to all the pumpkins on the front porch.

"Why does she have jack-o-lanterns out in January?"

"Halloween is Aunt Matilda's favorite holiday," I explained. "Besides, she says the jack-o-lanterns scare off the ghosts."

"Ghosts!" Josie backed up towards the gate.

"Yeah, ghosts! Real ones. Maybe you'll meet one!" Josie was a scaredy cat, too.

She must have read my mind. "I'm not afraid of anything," she said. "Let's go."

I knocked on the door.

"Tommy! Hello, hello, hello!" Aunt Matilda held a burning sparkler. Josie laughed.

"Just testing out my Fourth of July supply," she said and gave Josie a big smile.

"Josie, I'd like you to meet my Aunt Matilda," I said.

"Josie, is that short for Josephine?"

"No, Josephina," Josie mumbled. She hated her name.

"What a beautiful name," said Aunt Matilda. "Shall I call you that?"

"No!" she yelled. Josie could be a real brat.

"Then Josie, it is," said Aunt Matilda with another big smile. "You must be hungry. How about a snack? I've just gotten some fresh chocolate-covered grasshoppers."

"Yum," said Josie. She shot me a dirty look.

I put a grasshopper in my mouth and bit it. Actually, it wasn't bad if you ignored the crunchy sounds. Josie didn't eat one. She just pretended to. Then she wrapped it in a wad of chewing gum and stuck it under the table. Luckily, Aunt Matilda didn't notice. She was too busy telling us about holding a koala bear in Australia.

"Traveling is my favorite thing to do," she said to Josie. "Josie, tell me, do you like to travel?"

"I guess so. But I've never been really far away. My family just goes to boring places, like Tommy's house." Josie gave me a big fake smile.

"Well, I'm going to fix that. Do you like to have fun?"

"Yes, I do."

"Good! I do, too." Then suddenly she put her head back and fell fast asleep.

"Must have jet lag," said Josie. "Now what?"

"Let's go up to the attic," I suggested. "My aunt has all kinds of cool stuff up there."

An Awesome Discovery

We ran up the stairs to the attic. It was dark and dusty and packed with mysterious objects.

Josie put on an African mask with gigantic eyes. I pulled out a long red velvet cape from a drawer and flung it around my shoulders.

"Your majesty," said Josie, bowing.

"Time to vacuum off that dusty carpet!" It was Aunt Matilda's voice.

We jumped. Aunt Matilda had come up the attic steps without a sound.

"I hate chores!" wailed Josie.

"Oh, Josie, not that kind of vacuuming." She almost giggled at the idea.

Josie put her hands on her hips and looked annoyed.

"Oh, Josie, I was just teasing you. Tommy, haven't you ever wondered how I travel to all those places?" asked Aunt Matilda.

"Yes!" I answered.

"A long time ago, when I was in Morocco—in Africa—I met a very old man who was selling rugs. Even though I had been to the marketplace many times, I had never seen him before. He was no taller than a small child, and he sat on a tall stack of rugs drinking a glass of orange tea. He was blind, but I got the feeling that he could see some things better than I could. We talked about traveling. He said the only way to know a country is to learn about its people. Then he told me to take the rug he was sitting on.

"I told him that I didn't want the rug. Even if I did want a carpet, I wouldn't buy that one. It was ripped and stained and not very nice at all. But he insisted that I have it, and he would take no money for it. So I took it. I never saw the old man again. When it was time to leave, I unrolled the rug. It was more colorful than I had remembered."

"Auntie, that's a good story, but it doesn't explain how you travel so much."

"Silly me," laughed Aunt Matilda. "I did forget one teeny part of the story. It's a magic carpet, of course."

"Of course," said Josie. She shot me another one of those looks.

Aunt Matilda picked up a rug that was rolled up in the corner. She took one end of the carpet and snapped it in the air. Suddenly the colors of the carpet came alive. The deep reds and blues glowed like sparkling jewels. When she let go of the carpet, it hovered over the floor and made a whirring sound!

"Wow!" Josie and I said at the same time. I had seen some cool things at Aunt Matilda's house, but I'd never seen anything like this.

"Shall we try it out?" asked Aunt Matilda.

"I don't know," said Josie. "My mother wants me home by five."

"We can be home by then." Aunt Matilda tapped the rug. Suddenly, a computer screen filled with swirling colors unfolded from the carpet.

"Now, where shall we go?" Auntie mumbled to herself as she touched the screen. "First, enter time. Two hours or less. Good. Next field: Festivals and holidays. Where... Hmm. I think we'll take some curiosity, a dash of courage, plenty of gratitude, and, last but not least, fun!"

"Curiosity, courage—those aren't places," said Josie as she crossed her arms over her chest.

"With these new magic carpets," explained Aunt Matilda, "you type in what you hope to find, and the carpet brings you to the places where you'll find it. Hop on, kids! It's much more comfy than coach class."

We jumped on board. We flew out the attic window. We flew over the treetops and past our school. We flew over everything we knew, and then it all disappeared.

Happy New Year

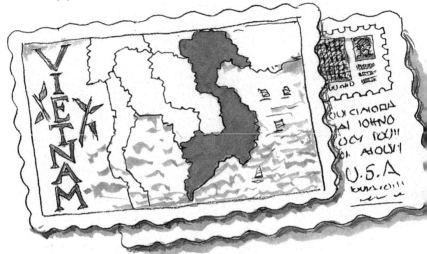

We landed in a green field. It was hot.

"Hurry," said Aunt Matilda. "We may be the first if we hurry." She ran toward a house, and we ran after her.

"The first what?" called Josie.

"The first guest, of course. In Vietnam, it's lucky to be the first visitor of the New Year."

We reached the house of Aunt Matilda's friends. They threw open the door and hugged her.

"Eat the Tet!" they said as they put rice cakes in our hands.

"Is this a Tet?" asked Josie as she unwrapped the rice cake.

"No, that's Banh chung, one of the traditional foods eaten during the Tet Festival. People say 'Eat the Tet' to celebrate all the good things that are coming in the year ahead," explained Aunt Matilda.

"Especially good food!" I said. "Wow, we're in Vietnam, about halfway around the world!"

"We also decorate our houses with peach blossoms," said the oldest child. She gave us each a branch with pink flowers on it.

"And have parades and fireworks," said another.

"And wear new clothes!" said the youngest.

"Tommy, don't look now, but I think your aunt has turned into a dragon," Josie said.

"Time for dragon dancing!" the dragon said in a muffled voice.

Josie and I put on the rest of the dragon costume. I held Aunt Matilda's waist and Josie held mine.

"I can't breathe and I can't see," Josie complained. "And is not exactly my idea of fun," mumbled Josie. Then she stepped on my toe.

I wanted to scream at her, but I kept my mouth shut.

BANG! BANG! BANG!

"Dragons under attack!" screamed Josie and fell to the ground.

"Silly, those are fireworks, which are another part of Tet," said Aunt Matilda.

We took off the dragon costume. The sky was full of sparkling light. I had never seen so many fireworks. Exactly at midnight, the fireworks ended.

"It's time to go," said Aunt Matilda.

The Festival of Color

We soared through the night, leaving the bright lights of Tet far behind us.

"Look, Mount Everest!" Aunt Matilda pointed. "The tallest mountain in the world!"

As we slid over Everest's peak, she shouted, "I hope you're not wearing your good clothes."

I looked down at my T-shirt and jeans. They weren't my good clothes, but they were the only clothes I had with me.

"Hold on, we're landing. India, here we come."

The carpet landed in a dusty street full of people with water pistols.

"Watch out, Josie!" I cried. But it was too late. She was dripping from head to foot with water that had been dyed bright green.

"Whaaa—" spluttered Josie.

Splat! Next thing I knew, someone had splashed red water all over me and Aunt Matilda. Aunt Matilda laughed and laughed as rivers of red water ran down her face.

"We're in Vrindavan, India, and just in time for the Festival of Color," said Aunt Matilda.

"India's so big that you can find a celebration practically every day of the year, but I think this festival is the most fun," she added.

Someone threw a handful of blue powder on me and ran away, laughing. Now I was red and blue.

"Why do they throw colors?" I asked. When I saw Josie, I started to laugh. She was green, yellow, purple and blue—and very angry.

"Because spring has arrived and it's time to take on the colors of spring flowers," said Aunt Matilda. "That powder is called gulal. Everyone—children and adults, rich and poor—throw gulal and water on each other during Holi. It's hard to be serious when you're every color of the rainbow!" Then she added, "C'mon, kids, let's find a bathtub and fly. We've got lots more to see and not much time to see it."

In the Land of Giants

"Bonjour, Douai!" said Aunt Matilda as we landed in a very old town. We were in the middle of a parade!

Brass bands marched around us. The music they played filled the air. Pigeons swooped through the sky. Tiny bits of confetti floated down. It stuck to our hair and clothes. Everyone around us was dancing and having fun.

"Yikes!" screamed Josie.

We were surrounded by giants! Small giants, medium giants, and some very tall giants were everywhere!

"Relax, Josie. They're puppets, huge puppets," said Aunt Matilda. "We are in France and this is the Festival of Giants. Every July, the giants of Douai live again."

She pointed out a family of giants. "Look, they are the most famous giants. That's Father Gayant, his wife Madame Gayant, and their three children, Jacquot, Filion and baby Binbin. Binbin is eleven feet tall."

"That's a big baby," I said, looking up at the giants.

"They say that if you kiss Binbin, you will always be a part of Douai," said Aunt Matilda. She stood on tippy toes and threw the baby giant a kiss. Binbin shook his rattle happily.

"Josie, remember the puppets we made last year in school?" I asked.

There was no answer. Josie was gone!

Josie had disappeared. We ran through the crowd of giants, dancers, and musicians, calling her name.

Suddenly, we heard her scream. She was running toward us holding something. As she got closer, I could see that it was Father Gayant's red wig. I looked up. The giant was bald!

"It fell off him," explained Josie. "I picked it up before anybody could step on it. Now what?"

"We have to get it back on his head," I said.

Aunt Matilda said, "I know what to do." She got on the magic carpet. "Hop on," she instructed. Then she steered us up to the bald giant's head. "Put it back on," she said.

Josie leaned over and placed the red wig carefully on the giant's head. She looked happy for the first time.

Aunt Matilda winked. "Now you're getting into the spirit," she said. "Hold on tight."

The carpet blasted through the clouds, and we were off again.

Yams! Yams! Yams!

Soon we were over Africa. The carpet landed in a village of round houses with straw roofs.

"We are outside of Lagos, the capital of Nigeria. This is one of many villages that celebrates the Yam Festival. Isn't it wonderful!" Aunt Matilda exclaimed. "A party for a potato, which is what a yam is, you know," she said.

"If we're at the Yam Festival, then this must be—" said Josie.

"August, and don't worry, your mother won't even notice that you've been gone for eight months!" said Aunt Matilda.

Everywhere we looked, people were eating yams—fried yams, yam cakes, and roasted, baked, and boiled yams. Soon we were, too.

"These taste a lot like the sweet potatoes we have at Thanksgiving," I said.

"Yes, they're alike. Here, everyone eat yams to give thanks for a good harvest season. The festival begins after the oldest man in the village eats the first yam. Eating the first yam of the new crop is a great honor," said Aunt Matilda.

"Yeah, and they're giving thanks just like we do at Thanksgiving" said Josie.

"I might have, I'm sure I have…" Aunt Matilda stopped talking. She began to dig through her pockets for something.

There's one more thing about Aunt Matilda that I forgot to mention. Her pockets are full of papers. Not newspapers—they're much too large. No, she keeps little pieces of paper. She writes down things on them that she wants to remember. She has papers to remind her of all kinds of things, like the directions to the pizza parlor, poems that she likes, and the birthdays of people she meets. Some people might call them clutter, but not Aunt Matilda. She says that she can't live without them.

"Here it is," she said and started to unfold it. It seemed to take her forever. She held up a piece of paper. "My all-time favorite yam recipe." She waved it in the air with a triumphant expression on her face.

Here's what the paper said:

Matilda's All-Time Favorite Baked Yams

- 3-5 yams or sweet potatoes
- Butter
- 1 cup applesauce
- $\frac{1}{4}$ teaspoon ground nutmeg

Peel and slice the yams into circles about $\frac{1}{2}$-inch thick. Place in a casserole dish. Spoon applesauce over the yams. Dot with butter. Sprinkle with nutmeg. Ask an adult to bake it for 45 minutes at 350° Fahrenheit.

Aunt Matilda read the whole recipe aloud. The way she read it, you would have thought she was reading the best story ever written.

"Sounds delicious," I said, trying to be polite. I looked over at Josie, expecting to see her shoot me another one of her famous looks, but she didn't seem to be paying attention. I wondered what she was thinking about now.

"And nutritious," said Aunt Matilda. She looked off at the horizon and then turned back to the two of us. "Oh dear, I hadn't realized how late it's getting. I'm sorry to say that it's time to go home."

I couldn't believe it. I tried to hide my disappointment, but there's no fooling Aunt Matilda. She saw right through me.

"Tommy," she said, "There will be other trips someday and—"

Before you could say "sweet potato pie," Josie jumped on the magic carpet. She tapped "GO!" on the computer screen and the carpet immediately rose into the sky.

Aunt Matilda and I stood there, speechless. I don't think that I've ever seen Aunt Matilda speechless before.

"I don't ever want to go home! I'm having too much fun," Josie yelled down to us.

And then she was gone. Again.

I spoke first. "Now what?"

"I have no idea," said Aunt Matilda.

What was happening to everybody? Josie having too much fun? Aunt Matilda speechless and without a clue? I was starting to get worried.

Luckily, Aunt Matilda recovered. "Wait a minute," she said. She dug around in her bag again and took out yet another little piece of paper. "I'd almost forgotten that I had this. The man who gave me the rug said to read this in an emergency," she explained. "And this is most definitely an emergency!"

Never in my life had I been so grateful that Aunt Matilda couldn't live without clutter.

She put on her glasses and read:

"If without you the carpet should fly,

Whistle three times into the sky.

If that doesn't work, which it does as a rule,

Prepare to take a long vacation from school."

Aunt Matilda and I looked up into the big blue African sky. Josie was still nowhere in sight.

"Well," Aunt Matilda said, looking at me. "We have one chance. We might as well take it, don't you think?"

"Let's do it," I said, trying to sound sure of myself. It was a little hard, though, forcing the words out around the lump in my throat.

We whistled as loudly as we could. Once, twice, three times. Nothing happened. I looked at Aunt Matilda who was smiling bravely. "Patience," she said.

All of a sudden, the wind started to blow. It was so strong that the trees began to shake. I grabbed Aunt Matilda's hand. If we were going to blow away, I wanted to be sure that we blew away together.

Then we heard a whooshing sound. Josie and the carpet appeared out of nowhere.

"What were you thinking?" I screamed at Josie. She was such a troublemaker!

"You worry too much," said Josie, putting a sickly sweet smile on her face. To make matters worse, she sat on the carpet looking as if she owned it.

"Don't you realize that—"

Aunt Matilda interrupted me. "Josie was bitten by the travel bug," she said kindly. "It happens all the time, Tommy."

"Yeah, Tommy, haven't you ever heard of the famous travel bug?" asked Josie.

Before I could open my mouth, Aunt Matilda said, "Now, you two, back to business. We need to hurry if we want to get back home in time."

"Do we really have to go?" asked Josie.

"Yes, my dear, I'm afraid that we do. Move over, Josie, I'm joining you." She jumped up onto the carpet and took command of the controls. I have to admit that it was really a relief to see her back in charge. "Hop up behind us now, Tommy."

I climbed on and looked around at the other two. They looked the way I felt. We were all pretty tired, but it was a nice kind of tired. It had been some trip!

Home Again

Thump! We were back in Aunt Matilda's attic. Dong! A clock chimed.

"Four thirty," said Aunt Matilda. "Right on time."

I looked at Josie, and she looked at me. Funny, something was different about her, but I couldn't tell what. Then I knew! Josie was smiling—a big, happy, real smile.

"I'm hungry!" said Josie.

"Me, too!" Aunt Matilda said. "What shall we have?"

"How about some of those chocolate-covered grasshoppers?" said Josie. "I think I'm ready to try something new." She winked.

"No problem!" said Aunt Matilda. And she winked back.